Create a network
by grouping
several Sky Suits
together

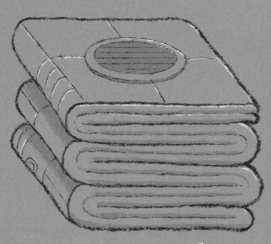

Folds up for
easy storage

| Not enough gas | Just right | Too much gas |

Sky Suits can be
built in a variety
of shapes and sizes

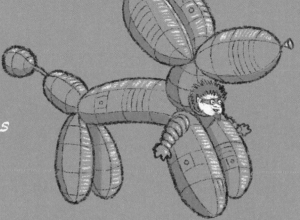

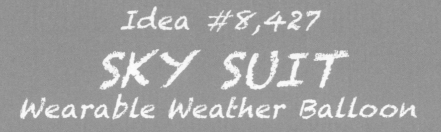

Idea #8,427
SKY SUIT
Wearable Weather Balloon

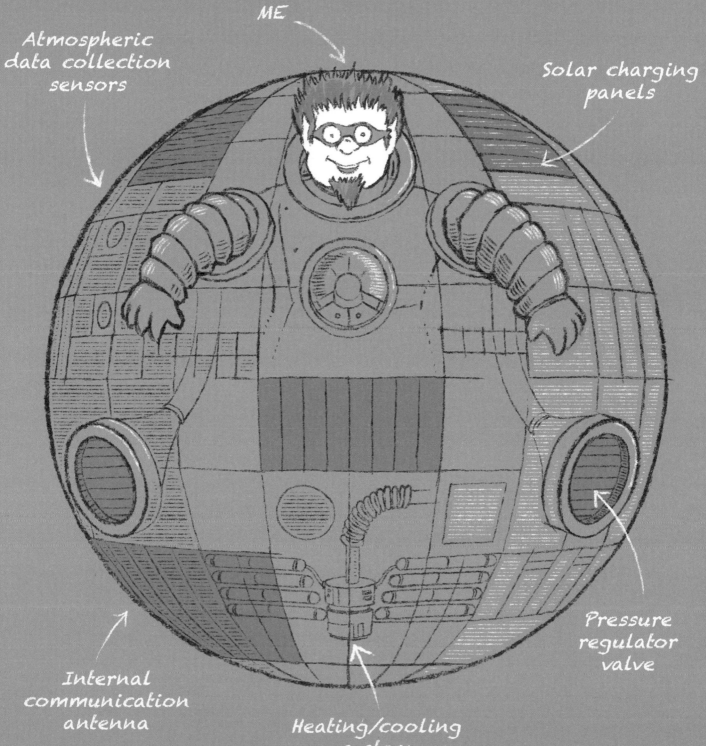

ME

Atmospheric data collection sensors

Solar charging panels

Internal communication antenna

Heating/cooling system

Pressure regulator valve

MAD SCIENTIST
ACADEMY

THE WEATHER DISASTER

MATTHEW McELLIGOTT

DRAGONFLY BOOKS ⟶ NEW YORK

**To Christy and Anthony,
and to Emily Easton, editor extraordinaire**

ACKNOWLEDGMENTS
Special thanks to stratospheric meteorologist
Jason Gough for his expert advice and guidance

All rights reserved. Published in the United States by Dragonfly Books, an imprint of Random House Children's Books, a division of Penguin Random House LLC, New York. Originally published in hardcover in the United States by Crown Books for Young Readers, New York, in 2016.

Dragonfly Books with the colophon is a registered trademark of Penguin Random House LLC.

Visit us on the Web! rhcbooks.com

Educators and librarians, for a variety of teaching tools, visit us at RHTeachersLibrarians.com

The Library of Congress has cataloged the hardcover edition of this work as follows:
Names: McElligott, Matthew.
Title: The weather disaster / Matthew McElligott.
Description: First Edition. | New York : Crown Books for Young Readers, [2016] | Series: Mad scientist academy
Identifiers: LCCN 2015024027 | ISBN 978-0-553-52376-8 (hardback) | ISBN 978-0-553-52379-9 (glb) | ISBN 978-0-553-52380-5 (ebook)
Subjects: LCSH: Severe storms—Juvenile literature. | Storms—Juvenile literature. | Floods—Juvenile literature.
Classification: LCC QC941.3 .M44 2016 | DDC 551.55—dc23

ISBN 978-0-553-52381-2 (pbk.)

The text of this book is set in Sunshine.
The illustrations were created with ink, pencil, and digital techniques.

MANUFACTURED IN CHINA
10 9 8 7 6 5 4 3 2 1
First Dragonfly Books Edition

Hey, Scarlet—the hygrometer shows the humidity is very high. There's a ton of water vapor in the air.

That makes sense. The handbook says that clouds form when warm, moist air rises and condenses.

THE WATER CYCLE

CONDENSATION

Cold temperatures higher in the atmosphere cause water vapor to condense into water droplets and ice crystals. This forms clouds.

EVAPORATION

Heat causes water vapor (moist air) to rise into the atmosphere.

PRECIPITATION

When so much water has condensed that the clouds cannot hold it anymore, the frozen or liquid water falls back to the earth.

If this condensation continues, it can even cause precipitation, like...

RAIN!

HOW A THUNDERSTORM FORMS

COLD AIR

ELECTRICAL CHARGE

WARM AIR

When enough warm, moist air keeps rising into the path of a cold, dry air mass, it can form a thunderstorm.

Water droplets and ice pellets get tossed up and down inside the cloud. This forms an electrical charge.

If the charge gets strong enough, it can be released to the ground as a bolt of lightning.

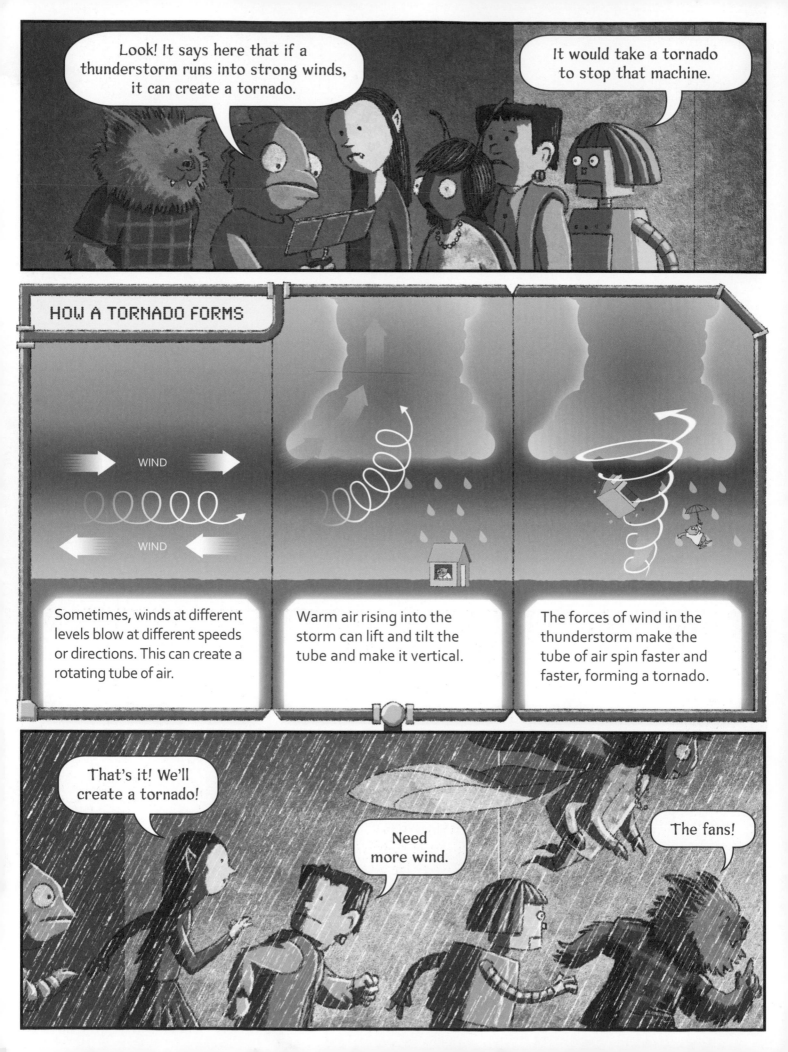

CLIMATE AND WEATHER

Dr. Cosmic,

Here are some notes about climate and weather you can share with your students.

-Prof. Nimbus

CLIMATE

CLIMATE IS THE AVERAGE PATTERN OF WEATHER IN A PLACE OVER MANY YEARS. FOR EXAMPLE, THE CLIMATE OF HAWAII IS WARM, BUT THE CLIMATE OF ANTARCTICA IS FREEZING COLD.

POLAR CLIMATE
(COOL TO VERY COLD ALL YEAR LONG)

TEMPERATE CLIMATE
(HOT IN SUMMER, COLD IN WINTER)

TROPICAL CLIMATE
(WARM TO HOT ALL YEAR LONG)

TEMPERATE CLIMATE
(HOT IN SUMMER, COLD IN WINTER)

POLAR CLIMATE
(COOL TO VERY COLD ALL YEAR LONG)

WEATHER SATELLITES

WEATHER SATELLITES ARE KEY TOOLS THAT SCIENTISTS USE TO STUDY WEATHER AND CLIMATE. THESE SPACECRAFT CIRCLE THE EARTH AND SEND BACK DATA ON CLOUDS AND STORMS, TEMPERATURES IN THE ATMOSPHERE, AND WIND SPEEDS.

For more weather facts, links, projects, and games, be sure to visit madscientistacademybooks.com.

WEATHER

WEATHER IS THE CONDITION OF THE ATMOSPHERE IN A PLACE OVER A SHORT PERIOD OF TIME. IT INCLUDES TEMPERATURE, WIND, CLOUDS, AND PRECIPITATION. WEATHER CAN BE VERY DIFFERENT IN NEARBY LOCATIONS ON THE SAME DAY. FOR EXAMPLE, IT MAY BE RAINING AT YOUR HOUSE, BUT SUNNY JUST A FEW MILES AWAY.

SUN	MON	TUE	WED	THU	FRI	SAT
82	86	84	81	80	84	87
60	63	61	58	57	60	63

Idea #8,513
CHAOS MACHINE
(Cooling/Heating Airflow Operating System)

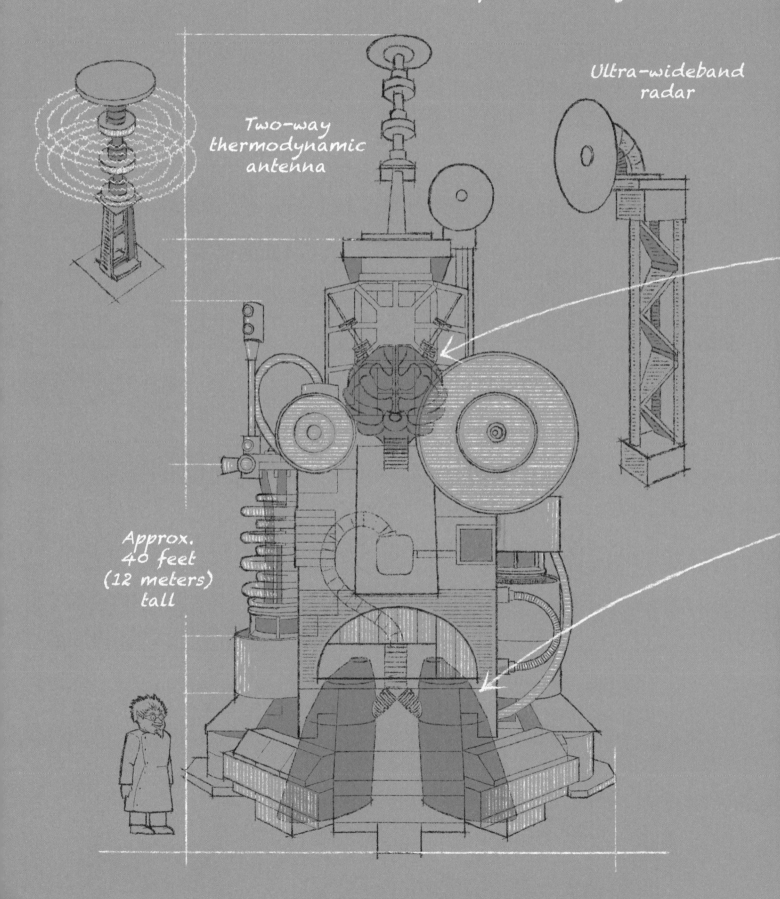

Two-way
thermodynamic
antenna

Ultra-wideband
radar

Approx.
40 feet
(12 meters)
tall

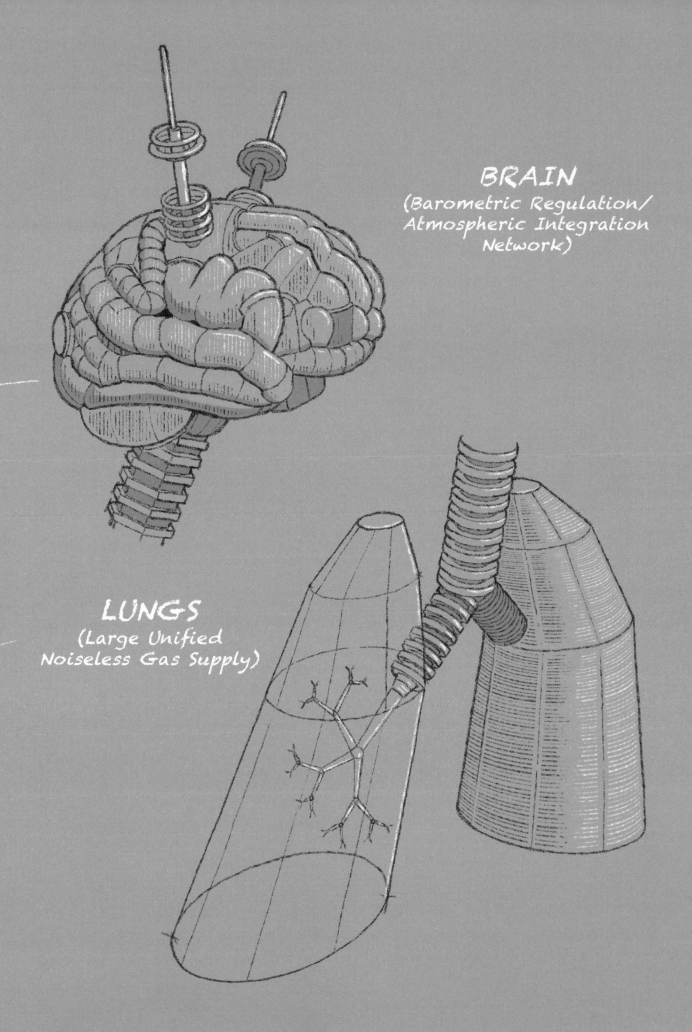

BRAIN
(Barometric Regulation/
Atmospheric Integration
Network)

LUNGS
(Large Unified
Noiseless Gas Supply)